For Alice, Archie and my
husband James – the
inspiration for 'Daddy'.
S H

For Tilly with love x.
N E

Sandy Creek
NEW YORK

An Imprint of Sterling Publishing Co., Inc.
1166 Avenue of the Americas
New York, NY 10036

Text © 2016 by Sam Hay
Illustrations © 2016 by Nick East

This 2016 edition published by Sandy Creek.

ISBN 978-1-4351-6399-7

Manufactured in Malaysia
Lot #:
10 9 8 7 6 5 4 3 2 1
03/16

DO NOT WASH THIS BEAR

by **Sam Hay**

Illustrated by **Nick East**

Sandy Creek
NEW YORK

My Daddy is not very good at doing the washing.

He shrinks my T-shirts.

He turns my vests pink.

And makes my socks **disappear**.

So when he wanted to wash Bear, I cried:

"No!"

But Daddy didn't listen.

"Bear smells," he said. "Bear is muddy and grubby and needs a clean!"

"Wait!" I said. And I showed Daddy the label under Bear's bottom.

DO NOT WASH THIS BEAR

But Daddy still didn't listen.

He popped Bear into the **washing machine**.

Bear whizzed and whirled.

Round and round.

Soapy and sloshy.

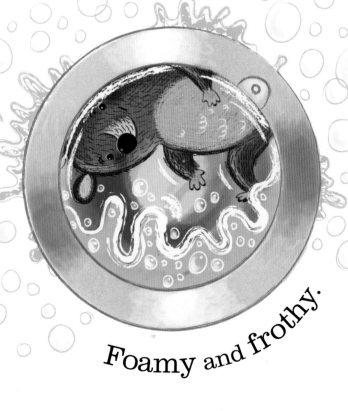

Foamy and frothy.

Then Daddy opened the door. Oh no!
Washing Bear was a big mistake . . .

Bear was different.
He **waved** at me.

He **winked**
at me.

He blew a **raspberry**!

"Look, Daddy!" I yelled. But Daddy was too busy looking for lost socks to see what Bear was up to.

Suddenly, Bear jumped out of the wash basket and ran up the stairs.

"Stop!" I said.

But Bear
didn't listen . . .

He bounced into the bathroom and started making bubbles.

Big bubbles.

"Stop!" I shouted.

But Bear didn't listen . . .

He ran into my bedroom
and made it snow.

Too much **snow!**

"Stop!
Achoo!"
I sneezed.

But Bear didn't listen . . .

Bear ran down the hall,
jumped on the cat and took
off down the stairs . . .

"Stop that **bear!**"
I hollered.

But Daddy
had so much
washing, he
couldn't see what
Bear was up to!

Just then the front
door opened.

"Mommy!"
I cried.

Mommy looked at Bear. Then she looked at Daddy and shook her head.

"You should have read the label!" she said.

DO NOT WASH THIS BEAR!

Mommy grabbed Bear
by the ears and
carried him, kicking
and grumbling, out
to the garden . . .

. . . and pegged him
on the line to dry.

Very soon, Bear was back to his old self again.
Daddy said Bear smelled better now.

But then he picked up Rabbit.

"Poo-eee," Daddy said. "Rabbit needs a wash!"

"NoooOOOOO!"

I shouted as I pointed to the label . . .